THE
SLIM PRINCESS

GEORGE ADE

The Slim Princess

George Ade

© 1st World Library – Literary Society, 2004
PO Box 2211
Fairfield, IA 52556
www.1stworldlibrary.org
First Edition

LCCN: 2004195298

Softcover ISBN: 1-4218-0129-9
Hardcover ISBN: 1-4218-0029-2
eBook ISBN: 1-4218-0229-5

Purchase *"The Slim Princess"*
as a traditional bound book at:
www.1stWorldLibrary.org/purchase.asp?ISBN=1-4218-0129-9

1st World Library Literary Society is a nonprofit organization dedicated to promoting literacy by:

- Creating a free internet library accessible from any computer worldwide.
- Hosting writing competitions and offering book publishing scholarships.

The Slim Princess
contributed by Tim, Ed & Rodney
in support of
1st World Library Literary Society

*   *   *   *   *

CONTENTS

I

WOMAN IN MOROVENIA

Morovenia is a state in which both the mosque and the motor-car now occur in the same landscape. It started out to be Turkish and later decided to be European.

The Mohammedan sanctuaries with their hideous stencil decorations and bulbous domes are jostled by many new shops with blinking fronts and German merchandise. The orthodox turn their faces toward Mecca while the enlightened dream of a journey to Paris. Men of title lately have made the pleasing discovery that they may drink champagne and still be good Mussulmans. The red slipper has been succeeded by the tan gaiter. The voluminous breeches now acknowledge the superior graces of intimate English trousers. Frock-coats are more conventional than beaded jackets. The fez remains as a part of the insignia of the old faith and hereditary devotion to the Sick Man.

The generation of males which has been extricating itself from the shackles of Orientalism has not devoted much worry to the Condition of Woman.

In Morovenia woman is still unliberated. She does not dine at a palm-garden or hop into a victoria on

Thursday afternoon to go to the meeting of a club organized to propagate cults. If she met a cult face to face she would not recognize it.

Nor does she suspect, as she sits in her prison apartment, peeping out through the lattice at the monotonous drift of the street life, that her sisters in far-away Michigan are organizing and raising missionary funds in her behalf.

She does not read the dressmaking periodicals. She never heard of the Wednesday matinée. When she takes the air she rides in a carriage that has a sheltering hood, and she is veiled up to the eyes, and she must never lean out to wriggle her little finger-tips at men lolling in front of the cafés. She must not see the men. She may look at them, but she must not see them. No wonder the sisters in Michigan are organizing to batter down the walls of tradition, and bring to her the more recent privileges of her sex!

Two years ago, when this story had its real beginning, the social status of woman in Morovenia was not greatly different from what it is to-day, or what it was two centuries ago.

Woman had two important duties assigned to her. One was to hide herself from the gaze of the multitude, and the other was to be beautiful - that is, fat. A woman who was plump, or buxom, or chubby might be classed as passably attractive, but only the fat women were irresistible. A woman weighing two hundred pounds was only two-thirds as beautiful as one weighing three hundred. Those grading below one hundred and fifty were verging upon the impossible.

II

KALORA'S AFFLICTION

If it had been planned to make this an old-fashioned discursive novel, say of the Victor Hugo variety, the second chapter would expend itself upon a philosophical discussion of Fat and a sensational showing of how and why the presence or absence of adipose tissue, at certain important crises, had altered the destinies of the whole race.

The subject offers vast possibilities. It involves the physical attractiveness of every woman in History and permits one to speculate wildly as to what might have happened if Cleopatra had weighed forty pounds heavier, if Elizabeth had been a gaunt and wiry creature, or if Joan of Arc had been so bulky that she could not have fastened on her armor.

The soft layers which enshroud the hard machinery of the human frame seem to arrive in a merely incidental or accidental sort of way. Yet once they have arrived they exert a mysterious influence over careers. Because of a mere change in contour, many a queen has lost her throne. It is a terrifying thought when one remembers that fat so often comes and so seldom goes.

It has been explained that in Morovenia, obesity and

feminine beauty increased in the same ratio. The woman reigning in the hearts of men was the one who could displace the most atmosphere.

Because of the fashionableness of fat, Count Selim Malagaski, Governor-General of Morovenia, was very unhappy. He had two daughters. One was fat; one was thin. To be more explicit, one was gloriously fat and the other was distressingly thin.

Jeneka was the name of the one who had been blessed abundantly. Several of the younger men in official circles, who had seen Jeneka at a distance, when she waddled to her carriage or turned side-wise to enter a shop-door, had written verses about her in which they compared her to the blushing pomegranate, the ripe melon, the luscious grape, and other vegetable luxuries more or less globular in form.

No one had dedicated any verses to Kalora. Kalora was the elder of the two. She had come to the alarming age of nineteen and no one had started in bidding for her.

In court circles, where there is much time for idle gossip, the most intimate secrets of an important household are often bandied about when the black coffee is being served. The marriageable young men of Morovenia had learned of the calamity in Count Malagaski's family. They knew that Kalora weighed less than one hundred and twenty pounds. She was tall, lithe, slender, sinuous, willowy, hideous. The fact that poor old Count Malagaski had made many unsucc-essful attempts to fatten her was a stock subject for jokes of an unrefined and Turkish character.

Whereas Jeneka would recline for hours at a time on a

shaded veranda, munching sugary confections that were loaded with nutritious nuts, Kalora showed a far-western preference for pickles and olives, and had been detected several times in the act of bribing servants to bring this contraband food into the harem.

Worse still, she insisted upon taking exercise. She loved to play romping games within the high walls of the inclosure where she and the other female attaches of the royal household were kept penned up. Her father coaxed, pleaded and even threatened, but she refused to lead the indolent life prescribed by custom; she scorned the sweet and heavy foods which would enable her to expand into loveliness; she persistently declined to be fat.

Kalora's education was being directed by a super-annuated professor named Popova. He was so antique and book-wormy that none of the usual objections urged against the male sex seemed to hold good in his case, and he had the free run of the palace. Count Selim Malagaski trusted him implicitly. Popova fawned upon the Governor-General, and seemed slavish in his devotion. Secretly and stealthily he was working out a frightful vengeance upon his patron. Twenty years before, Count Selim, in a moment of anger, had called Popova a "Christian dog."

In Morovenia it is flattery to call a man a "liar." It is just the same as saying to him, "You belong in the diplomatic corps." It is no disgrace to be branded as a thief, because all business transactions are saturated with treachery. But to call another a "Christian dog" is the thirty-third degree of insult.

Popova writhed in spirit when he was called

"Christian," but he covered his wrath and remained in the nobleman's service and waited for his revenge. And now he was sacrificing the innocent Kalora in order to punish the father. He said to himself: "If she does not fatten, then her father's heart will be broken, and he will suffer even as I have suffered from being called Christian."

It was Popova who, by guarded methods, encouraged her to violent exercise, whereby she became as hard and trim as an antelope. He continued to supply her with all kinds of sour and biting foods and sharp mineral waters, which are the sworn enemies of any sebaceous condition. And now that she was nineteen, almost at the further boundary of the marrying age, and slimmer than ever before, he rejoiced greatly, for he had accomplished his deep and malign purpose, and laid a heavy burden of sorrow upon Count Selim Malagaski.

III

THE CRUELTY OF LAW

If the father was worried by the prolonged crisis, the younger sister, Jeneka, was well-nigh distracted, for she could not hope to marry until Kalora had been properly mated and sent away.

In Morovenia there is a very strict law intended to eliminate the spinster from the social horizon. It is a law born of craft and inspired by foresight. The daughters of a household must be married off in the order of their nativity. The younger sister dare not contemplate matrimony until the elder sister has been led to the altar. It is impossible for a young and attractive girl to make a desirable match leaving a maiden sister marooned on the market. She must cooperate with her parents and with the elder sister to clear the way.

As a rule this law encourages earnest getting-together in every household and results in a clearing up of the entire stock of eligible daughters. But think of the unhappy lot of an adorable and much-coveted maiden who finds herself wedged in behind something unattractive and shelf-worn! Jeneka was thus pocketed. She could do nothing except fold her hands and patiently wait for some miraculous intervention.

In Morovenia the discreet marrying age is about sixteen. Jeneka was eighteen - still young enough and of a most ravishing weight, but the slim princess stood as a slight, yet seemingly insurmountable barrier between her and all hopes of conventional happiness.

Count Malagaski did not know that the shameful fact of Kalora's thinness was being whispered among the young men of Morovenia. When the daughters were out for their daily carriage-ride both wore flowing robes. In the case of Kalora, this augmented costume was intended to conceal the absence of noble dimensions.

It is not good form in Morovenia for a husband or father to discuss his home life, or to show enthusiasm on the subject of mere woman; but the Count, prompted by a fretful desire to dispose of his rapidly maturing offspring, often remarked to the high-born young gentlemen of his acquaintance that Kalora was a most remarkable girl and one possessed of many charms, leaving them to infer, if they cared to do so, that possibly she weighed at least one hundred and eighty pounds.

These casual comments did not seem to arouse any burning curiosity among the young men, and up to the day of Kalora's nineteenth anniversary they had not had the effect of bringing to the father any of those guarded inquiries which, under the oriental custom, are always preliminary to an actual proposal of marriage.

Count Selim Malagaski had a double reason for wishing to see Kalora married. While she remained at home he knew that he would be second in authority. There is an occidental misapprehension to the effect that every woman beyond the borders of the Levant is a languorous and waxen lily, floating in a milk-warm pool of idleness. It is true that the women of a household live in certain apartments set aside as a "harem." But "harem" literally means "forbidden" - that is, forbidden to the public, nothing more. Every villa at Newport has a "harem."

The women of Morovenia do not pour tea for men every afternoon, and they are kept well under cover, but they are not slaves. They do not inherit a nominal authority, but very often they assume a real authority. In the United States, women can not sail a boat, and yet they direct the cruise of the yacht. Railway presidents can not vote in the Senate, and yet they always know how the votes are going to be cast. And in Morovenia, many a clever woman, deprived of specified and legal rights, has learned to rule man by those tactful methods which are in such general use that they need not be specified in this connection.

Kalora had a way of getting around her father. After she had defied him and put him into a stewing rage, she would smooth him the right way and, with teasing little cajoleries, nurse him back to a pleasant humor. He would find himself once more at the starting-place of the controversy, his stern commands unheeded, and the disobedient daughter laughing in his very face.

Thus, while he was ashamed of her physical imperfections, he admired her cleverness. Often he said to Popova: "I tell you, she might make some man a sprightly and entertaining companion, even if she *is* slender."

Whereupon the crafty Popova would reply: "Be

patient, your Excellency. We shall yet have her as round as a dumpling."

And all the time he was keeping her trained as fine as the proverbial fiddle.

IV

THE GARDEN PARTY

Said the Governor-General to himself in that prime hour for wide-awake meditation - the one just before arising for breakfast: "She is not all that she should be, and yet, millions of women have been less than perfect and most of them have married."

He looked hard at the ceiling for a full minute and then murmured, "Even men have their shortcomings."

This declaration struck him as being sinful and almost infidel in its radicalism, and yet it seemed to open the way to a logical reason why some titled bachelor of damaged reputation and tottering finances might balance his poor assets against a dowry and a social position, even though he would be compelled to figure Kalora into the bargain.

It must be known that the Governor-General was now simply looking for a husband for Kalora. He did not hope to top the market or bring down any notable catch. He favored any alliance that would result in no discredit to his noble lineage.

"At present they do not even nibble," he soliloquized, still looking at the ceiling. "They have taken fright for some reason. They may have an inkling of the awful truth. She is nineteen. Next year she will be twenty - the year after that twenty-one. Then it would be too late. A desperate experiment is better than inaction. I have much to gain and nothing to lose. I must exhibit Kalora. I shall bring the young men to her. Some of them may take a fancy to her. I have seen people eat sugar on tomatoes and pepper on ice-cream. There may be in Morovenia one - one would be sufficient - one bachelor who is no stickler for full-blown loveliness. I may find a man who has become inoculated with western heresies and believes that a woman with intellect is desirable, even though under weight. I may find a fool, or an aristocrat who has gambled. I may stumble upon good fortune if I put her out among the young men. Yes, I must exhibit her, but how - how?"

He began reaching into thin air for a pretext and found one. The inspiration was simple and satisfying.

He would give a garden-party in honor of Mr. Rawley Plumston, the British Consul. Of course he would have to invite Mrs. Plumston and then, out of deference to European custom, he would have his two daughters present. It was only by the use of imported etiquette that he could open the way to direct courtship.

Possibly some of the cautious young noblemen would talk with Kalora, and, finding her bright-eyed, witty, ready in conversation and with enthusiasm for big and masculine undertakings, be attracted to her. At the same time her father decided that there was no reason why her pitiful shortage of avoirdupois should be candidly advertised. Even at a garden-party, where the guests of honor are two English subjects, the young women would be required to veil themselves up to the nose-tips and hide themselves within a veritable cocoon of soft garments.

The invitations went out and the acceptances came in. The English were flattered. Count Malagaski was buoyed by new hopes and the daughters were in a day-and-night flutter, for neither of them had ever come within speaking distance of the real young man of their dreams.

On the morning of the day set apart for the début of Kalora, Count Selim went to her apartments, and, with a rather shamefaced reluctance, gave his directions.

"Kalora, I have done all for you that any father could do for a beloved child and you are still thin," he began.

"Slender," she corrected.

"Thin," he repeated. "Thin as a crane - a mere shadow of a girl - and, what is more deplorable, apparently indifferent to the sorrow that you are causing those most interested in your welfare."

"I am not indifferent, father. If, merely by wishing, I could be fat, I would make myself the shape of the French balloon that floated over Morovenia last week. I would be so roly-poly that, when it came time for me to go and meet our guests this afternoon, I would roll into their presence as if I were a tennis-ball."

"Why should you know anything about tennis-balls? You, of all the young women in Morovenia, seem to be the only one with a fondness for athletics. I have heard that in Great Britain, where the women ride and play rude, manly games, there has been developed a breed as hard as flint - Allah preserve me from such women!"

"Father, you are leading up to something. What is it you wish to say?"

"This. You have persistently disobeyed me and made me very unhappy, but to-day I must ask you to respect my wishes. Do not proclaim to our guests the sad truth regarding your deficiency."

"Good!" she exclaimed gaily. "I shall wear a robe the size of an Arabian tent, and I shall surround myself with soft pillows, and I shall wheeze when I breathe and - who knows? - perhaps some dark-eyed young man worth a million piasters will be deceived, and will come to you to-morrow, and buy me - buy me at so much a pound." And she shrieked with laughter.

"Stop!" commanded her father. "You refuse to take me seriously, but I am in earnest. Do not humiliate me in the presence of my friends this afternoon."

Then he hurried away before she had time to make further sport of him.

To Count Selim Malagaski this garden-party was the frantic effort of a sinking man. To Kalora it was a lark. From the pure fun of the thing, she obeyed her father. She wore four heavily quilted and padded gowns, one over another, and when she and Jeneka were summoned from their apartments and went out to meet the company under the trees, they were almost like twins and both duck-like in general outlines.

First they met Mrs. Rawley Plumston, a very tall, bony

and dignified woman in gray, wearing a most flowery hat. To every man of Morovenia Mrs. Plumston was the apotheosis of all that was undesirable in her sex, but they were exceedingly polite to her, for the reason that Morovenia owed a great deal of money in London and it was a set policy to cultivate the friendship of the British.

While Jeneka and Kalora were being presented to the consul's wife, these same young men, the very flower of bachelorhood, stood back at a respectful distance and regarded the young women with half-concealed curiosity. To be permitted to inspect young women of the upper classes was a most unusual privilege, and they knew why the privilege had been extended to them. It was all very amusing, but they were too well bred to betray their real emotions. When they moved up to be presented to the sisters they seemed grave in their salutations and restrained themselves, even though one pair of eyes, peering out above a very gauzy veil, seemed to twinkle with mischief and to corroborate their most pronounced suspicions.

Out of courtesy to his guests, Count Malagaski had made his garden-party as deadly dull as possible. Little groups of bored people drifted about under the trees and exchanged the usual commonplace observations. Tea and cakes were served under a canopy tent and the local orchestra struggled with pagan music.

Kalora found herself in a wide and easy kind of a basket-chair sitting under a tree and chatting with Mrs. Plumston. She was trying to be at her ease, and all the time she knew that every young man present was staring at her out of the corner of his eye.

Mrs. Plumston, although very tall and evidently of brawny strength, had a twittering little voice and a most confiding manner. She was immensely interested in the daughter of the Governor-General. To meet a young girl who had spent her life within the mysterious shadows of an oriental household gave her a tingling interest, the same as reading a forbidden book. She readily won the confidence of Kalora, and Kalora, being most ingenuous and not educated to the wiles of the drawing-room, spoke her thoughts with the utmost candor.

"I like you," she said to Mrs. Plumston, "and, oh, how I envy you! You go to balls and dinners and the theater, don't you?"

"Alas, yes, and you escape them! How I envy *you*!"

"Your husband is a very handsome man. Do you love him?"

"I tolerate him."

"Does he ever scold you for being thin?"

"Does he *what*?"

"Is he ever angry with you because you are not big and plump and - and - pulpy?"

"Heavens, no! If my husband has any private convictions regarding my personal appearance, he is discreet enough to keep them to himself. If he isn't satisfied with me, he should be. I have been working for years to save myself from becoming fat and plump and - pulpy."

"Then you don't think fat women are beautiful?"

"My child, in all enlightened countries adipose is woman's worst enemy. If I were a fat woman, and a man said that he loved me, I should know that he was after my bank-account. Take my advice, my dear young lady, and bant."

"Bant?"

"Reduce. Make yourself slender. You have beautiful eyes, beautiful hair, a perfect complexion, and with a trim figure you would be simply incomparable."

Kalora listened, trembling with surprise and pleasure. Then she leaned over and took the hand of the gracious Englishwoman.

"I have a confession to make," she said in a whisper. "I am not fat - I am slim - quite slim."

And then, at that moment, something happened to make this whole story worth telling. It was a little something, but it was the beginning of many strange experiences, for it broke up the wonderful garden-party in the grounds of the Governor-General, and it gave Morovenia something to talk about for many weeks to come. It all came about as follows:

At the military club, the night before the party, a full score of young men, representing the quality, sat at an oblong table and partook of refreshments not sanctioned by the Prophet. They were young men of registered birth and supposititious breeding, even though most of them had very little head back of the ears and wore the hair clipped short and were big of bone, like work-horses, and had the gusty manners of the camp.

They were foolishly gloating over the prospect of meeting the two daughters of the Governor-General, and were telling what they knew about them with much freedom, for, even in a monarchy, the chief executive and his family are public property and subject to the censorship of any one who has a voice for talking.

Of these male gossips there were a few who said, with gleeful certainty, that the elder daughter was a mere twig who could hide within the shadow of her bounteous and incomparable sister.

"Wait until to-morrow and you shall see," they said, wagging their heads very wisely.

To-morrow had come and with it the party and here was Kalora - a pretty face peering out from a great pod of clothes.

They stood back and whispered and guessed, until one, more enterprising than the others, suggested a bold experiment to set all doubts at rest.

Count Malagaski had provided a diversion for his guests. A company of Arabian acrobats, on their way from Constantinople to Paris, had been intercepted, and were to give an exhibition of leaping and pyramid-building at one end of the garden. While Kalora was chatting with Mrs. Plumston, the acrobats had entered and, throwing off their yellow-and-black striped gowns, were preparing for the feats. They were behind the two women and at the far end of the garden. Mrs.

Plumston and Kalora would have to move to the other side of the tree in order to witness the exhibition. This fact gave the devil-may-care young bachelors a ready excuse.

"Do as I have directed and you shall learn for yourselves," said the one who had invented the tactics. "I tell you that what you see is all shell. Now then -"

Four conspirators advanced in a half-careless and sauntering manner to where Kalora and the consul's wife sat by the sheltering tree, intent upon their exchange of secrets.

"Pardon me, Mrs. Plumston, but the acrobats are about to begin," said one of the young men, touching the fez with his forefinger.

"Oh, really?" she exclaimed, looking up. "We must see them."

"You must face the other way," said the young man. "They are at the east end of the garden. Permit us."

Whereupon the young man who had spoken and a companion who stood at his side very gently picked up Mrs. Plumston's big basket-chair between them and carried it around to the other side of the tree. And the two young men who had been waiting just behind picked up Kalora's chair and carried *her* to the other side of the tree, and put her down beside the consul's wife.

Did they carry her? No, they dandled her. She was as light as a feather for these two young giants of the military. They made a palpable show of the ridiculous ease with which they could lift their burden. It may have been a forward thing to do, but they had done it with courtly politeness, and the consul's wife, instead of being annoyed, was pleased and smiling over the very pretty little attention, for she could not know at the moment that the whole maneuver had grown out of a wager and was part of a detestable plan to find out the actual weight of the Governor-General's elder daughter.

If Mrs. Plumston did not understand, Count Selim Malagaski understood. So did all the young men who were watching the pantomime. And Kalora understood. She looked up and saw the lurking smiles on the faces of the two gallants who were carrying her, and later the tittering became louder and some of the young men laughed aloud.

She leaped from her chair and turned upon her two tormentors.

"How dare you?" she exclaimed. "You are making sport of me in the presence of my father's guests! You have a contempt for me because I am ugly. You mock at me in private because you hear that I am thin. You wish to learn the truth about me. Well, I will tell you. I *am* thin. I weigh one hundred and eighteen pounds."

She was speaking loudly and defiantly, and all the young men were backing away, dismayed at the outbreak. Her father elbowed his way among them, white with terror, and attempted to pacify her.

"Be still, my child!" he commanded. "You don't know what you are saying!"

"Yes, I do know what I am saying!" she persisted, her voice rising shrilly. "Do they wish to know about me? Must they know the truth? Then look! *Look*!"

With sweeping outward gestures she threw off the soft quilted robes gathered about her, tore away the veil and stood before them in a white gown that fairly revealed every modified in-and-out of her figure.

What ensued? Is it necessary to tell? The costume in which she stood forth was no more startling or immodest than the simple gown which the American high-school girl wears on her Commencement Day, and it was decidedly more ample than the sum of all the garments worn at polite social gatherings in communities somewhat to the west. Nevertheless, the company stood aghast. They were doubly horrified - first, at the effrontery of the girl, and second, at the revelation of her real person, for they saw that she was doomed, helpless, bereft of hope, slim beyond all curing.

V

HE ARRIVES

Kalora was alone.

After putting the company to consternation she had flung herself defiantly back into the chair and directed a most contemptuous gaze at all the desirable young men of her native land.

The Governor-General made a choking attempt to apologize and explain, and then, groping for an excuse to send the people away, suggested that the company view the new stables. The acrobats were dismissed. The guests went rapidly to an inspection of the carriages and horses. They were glad to escape. Jeneka, crushed in spirit and shamed at the brazen performance of her sister, began a plaintive conjecture as to "what people would say," when Kalora turned upon her such a tigerish glance that she fairly ran for her apartment, although she was too corpulent for actual sprinting. Mrs. Plumston remained behind as the only comforter.

"It was a most contemptible proceeding, my child. When they lifted us and carried us to the other side of the tree I thought it was rather nice of them; something on the order of the old Walter Raleigh days of chivalry, and all that. And just think! The beasts did it to find out whether or not you were really plump and heavy. It's a most extraordinary incident."

"I wouldn't marry one of them now, not if he begged and my father commanded!" said Kalora bitterly. "And poor Jeneka! This takes away her last chance. Until I am married she can not marry, and after to-day not even a blind man would choose me."

"For goodness' sake, don't worry! You tell me you are nineteen. No woman need feel discouraged until she is about thirty-five. You have sixteen years ahead of you."

"Not in Morovenia."

"Why remain in Morovenia?"

"We are not permitted to travel."

"Perhaps, after what happened to-day, your father will be glad to let you travel," said Mrs. Plumston with a significant little nod and a wise squint. "Don't you generally succeed in having your own way with him?"

"Oh, to travel - to travel!" exclaimed Kalora, clasping her hands. "If I am to remain single and a burden for ever, perhaps it would lighten father's grief if I resided far away. My presence certainly would remind him of the wreck of all his ambitions, but if I should settle down in Vienna or Paris, or -" she paused and gave a little gasp -" or if anything should happen to me, if I should - should disappear, that is, really disappear, Jeneka would be free to marry and -"

"Oh, pickles!" said Mrs. Plumston. "I have heard of romantic young women jumping overboard and taking poison on account of rich young men, but I never heard of a girl's snuffing herself out so as to give her sister a chance to get married. The thing for you to do at a time like this, when you find yourself in a tangle, is to think of yourself and your own chances for happiness. Father and Jeneka will take care of themselves. They are popular and beloved characters here in Morovenia. They are not taking you into consideration except as you seem to interfere with their selfish plans. I have made it a rule not to work out my neighbor's destiny."

"What can I do?" asked Kalora, seemingly impressed by the earnestness of the consul's wife.

"Leave Morovenia. Keep at your father until he consents to your going. Here you are despised and ridiculed - a victim of heathen prejudice left over from the Dark Ages. Get away, even if you have to walk, and take my word for it, the moment you leave Morovenia you will be a very beautiful girl; not a merely attractive young person, but what we would call at home a radiant beauty - the oriental type, you know. And as a personal favor to me, don't be fat."

"No fear of that," said the girl with a melancholy attempt at a smile. "But you must go and join the others. Do, please. I am now in disgrace, and you may compromise your social standing in Morovenia if you remain here and talk to me."

"I dare say I should go. I have a husband who requires as much attention and scolding as a four-year-old. Sometimes I almost favor the oriental system of the husband's directing the wife. Good-by."

"Good-by."

Mrs. Plumston gave her a kiss and a friendly little pat on the arm, and walked away toward the stables with a swinging, heel-and-toe, masculine stride.

Kalora had the whole garden to herself. She sat squared up in the wicker chair with her fists clenched, looking straight ahead, trying in vain to think of some plan for avenging herself upon the whole race of bachelors. As she sat thus some one spoke to her.

"How do you do?" came a voice.

She was startled and looked about, but saw no one.

"Up here!" came the voice again.

She looked up and saw a young man on the top of the wall, his legs hanging over. Evidently he had climbed up from the outside, and yet Kalora had never suspected that the wall could be climbed.

He was smoothly shaven, with blond hair almost ripe enough to be auburn; he wore a gray suit of rather loose and careless material, a belt, but no waistcoat; his trousers were reefed up from a pair of saddle-brown shoes, and the silk band around his small straw hat was tricolored. In his hand was a paper-covered book. Swung over his shoulder was a camera in a leather case. He sat there on top of the high wall and gazed at Kalora with a grinning interest, and she, forgetting that she was unveiled and clad only in the simple garments which had horrified the best people of Morovenia, gazed back at him, for he was the first of the kind she had seen.

"What are you doing here?" she asked wonderingly.

"I am looking for the show," he replied. "They told me down at the hotel that a very hot bunch of acrobats were doing a few stunts down here this afternoon, and I thought I'd break in if I could. Wanted to get some pictures of them."

"Were you invited?"

"No, but that doesn't make any difference. In Cairo I went to a native wedding every day. If I passed a house where there was a wedding being pulled off, I simply went inside and mingled. They never put me out - seemed to enjoy having me there. I suppose they thought it was the American custom for outsiders to ring in at a wedding."

"You said American, didn't you? Are you from America?"

"Do I look like a Scandinavian? I am from the grand old commonwealth of Pennsylvania. Did you ever hear of the town of Bessemer?"

"I'm afraid not."

"Did you ever hear of the Pike family that robbed all the orphans, tore down the starry banner, walked on the humble working-girl and gave the double cross to the common people? Did you?"

"Dear me, no," she replied, following him vaguely.

"Well, I am Alexander H., of the tribe of Pike, and I have two reasons for being in your beautiful little city.

One is Federal grand jury and the other is ten-cent magazine. You know, our folks are sinfully rich. About four years ago I came in for most of the guvnor's coin, and in trying to keep up the traditions of the family, I have made myself unpopular, but I didn't know how unpopular I really was until I got this magazine from home this morning." And he held up the paper-covered book, which had a rainbow cover. "They have been writing up a few of us captains of industry, and they have said everything about me that they *could* say without having the thing barred out of the mails. I notice that you speak our kind of talk fairly well, but I think I can take you by the hand and show you a lot of new and beautiful English language. I will read this to you."

Before she could warn him, or do anything except let out a horrified "Oh-h!" he had leaped lightly from his high perch and was standing in front of her.

"I'm afraid you don't understand," she said, rising and taking a frightened survey of the garden, to be sure that no one was watching. "Strangers are not permitted in here. That is, men, and more especially - ah - Christians."

"I'm not a Christian, and I can prove it by this magazine. I am an octopus, and a viper, and a vampire, and a man-eating shark. I am what you might call a composite zoo. If you want to get a line on me just read this article on *The Shameless Brigand of Bessemer*, and you will certainly find out that I am a nice young fellow."

Kalora had studied English for years and thought she knew it, and yet she found it difficult fully, to comprehend all the figurative phrases of this pleasing young stranger.

"Do I understand that you are traveling abroad because of your unpopularity at home?" she asked.

"I am waiting for things to cool down. As soon as the muck-rakers wear out their rakes, and the great American public finds some other kind of hysterics to keep it worked up to a proper temperature, I shall mosey back and resume business at the old stand. But why tell you the story of my life? Play fair now, and tell me a lot about yourself. Where am I?"

"You are here in my father's private garden, where you hare no right to be."

"And father?"

"Is Count Selim Malagaski, Governor-General of Morovenia."

"Wow! And you?"

"I am his daughter."

"The daughter of all that must be something. Have you a title?"

"I am called Princess."

"Can you beat that? Climb up a wall to see some A-rabs perform, and find a real, sure-enough princess, and likewise, if you don't mind my saying so, a pippin."

"I don't know what you mean," she said.

"A corker."

"Corker?"

"I mean that you're a good-looker - that it's no labor at all to gaze right at you. I didn't think they grew them so far from headquarters, but I see I'm wrong. You are certainly all right. Pardon me for saying this to you so soon after we meet, but I have learned that you will never break a woman's heart by telling her that she is a beaut."

Kalora leaned back in her chair and laughed. She was beginning to comprehend the whimsical humor of the very unusual young man. His direct and playful manner of speech amused her, and also seemed to reassure her. And, when he seated himself within a few inches of her elbow, fanning himself with the little straw hat, and calmly inspecting the tiny landscape of the forbidden garden, she made no protest against his familiarity, although she knew that she was violating the most sacred rules laid down for her sex.

She reasoned thus with herself:

"To-day I have disgraced myself to the utmost, and, since I am utterly shamed, why not revel in my lawlessness?"

Besides, she wished to question this young man. Mrs. Plumston had said to her: "You are beautiful." No one else had ever intimated such a thing. In fact, for five years she had been taunted almost daily because of her lack of all physical charms. Perhaps she could learn the truth about herself by some adroit questioning of the young man from Pennsylvania.

"You have traveled a great deal?" she asked.

"Me and Baedeker and Cook wrote it," he replied; and then, seeing that she was puzzled, he said: "I have been to all of the places they keep open."

"You have seen many women in many countries?"

"I have. I couldn't help it, and I'm glad of it."

"Then you know what constitutes beauty?"

"Not always. What is sponge cake for me may be sawdust for somebody else. Say, I rode for an hour in a 'rickshaw at Nagoya to see the most beautiful girl in Japan and when we got to the teahouse they trotted out a little shrimp that looked as if she'd been dried over a barrel - you know, stood *bent* all the time, as if she was getting ready to jump. Her neck was no bigger than a gripman's wrist and she had a nose that stood right out from her face almost an eighth of an inch. Her eyes were set on the bias and she was painted more colors than a bandwagon. I said, 'If this is the champion geisha, take me back to the land of the chorus girl.' And in China! Listen! I caught a Chinese belle coming down the Queen's Road in Hong-Kong one day, and I ran up an alley. I have seen Parisian beauties that had a coat of white veneering over them an inch thick, and out here in this country I have seen so-called cracker-jacks that ought to be doing the mountain-of-flesh act in the Ringling side-show. So there you are!"

"But in your own country, and in the larger cities of the

world, there must be some sort of standard. What are the requirements? What must a woman be, that all men would call her beautiful?"

"Well, Princess, that's a pretty hard proposition to dope out. Good looks can not be analyzed in a lab or worked out by algebra, because, I'm telling you, the one that may look awful lucky to me may strike somebody else as being fairly punk. Providence framed it up that way so as to give more girls a chance to land somebody. Still, there is one kind that makes a hit wherever people are bright enough to sit up and take notice. Now I suppose that any male being in his right senses would find it easy to look at a woman who was young enough and had eyes and hair and teeth and the other items, all doing team-work together, and then if she was trim and slender -"

"Should she be slender?" interrupted Kalora, leaning toward him.

"Sure. I don't mean the same width all the way up and down, like an art student, but trim and - Here, I'll show you. You will find the pictures of the most beautiful women in the world right here in the ads of a ten-cent magazine. Look them over and you will understand what I mean."

He turned page after page and showed her the tapering goddesses of the straight front, the tooth-powder, the camera, the breakfast-food, the massage-cream, and the hair-tonic.

"These are what you call beautiful women?" she asked.

"These are about the limit."

"Then in your country I would not be considered hideous, would I?"

"Hideous? Say, if you ever walked up Fifth Avenue you would block the traffic! And in the palm-garden at the Waldorf - why, you and the head waiter would own the place! Are you trying to string me by asking such questions? Are you a real ingénue, or a kidder?"

"I hardly know what you mean, but I assure you that here in Morovenia they laugh at me because I am not fat."

"This is a shine country, and you're in wrong, little girl," said Mr. Pike, in a kindly tone. "Why don't you duck?"

"Duck?"

"Leave here and hunt up some of the red spots on the map. You know what I mean - away to the bright lights! I don't like to knock your native land but, honestly, Morovenia is a bad boy. I've struck towns around here where you couldn't buy illustrated post-cards. They take in the sidewalks at nine o'clock every night. That orchestra down at the hotel handed me a new coon song last night - *Bill Bailey*! Can you beat that? As long as you stay here you are hooked up with a funeral."

Kalora, with wrinkled brow, had been striving to follow him in his figurative flights.

"Strange," she murmured. "You are the second person I have met to-day who advises me to go away - to the west."

"That's the tip!" he exclaimed with fervor. "Go west and when you start, keep on going. You come to America and bring along the papers to show that you're a real live princess and you'll own both sides of the street. We'll show you more real excitement in two weeks than you'll see around here if you live to be a hundred."

"I should like to go, but - Look! Hurry, please! You must go!"

She pointed, and young Mr. Pike turned to see two guards in baggy uniforms bearing down upon him, their eyes bulging with amazement.

"Shall I try to put up a bluff, or fight it out?" he asked, as he stood up to meet them.

"You can not explain," gasped Kalora. "Run! *Run!* They know you have no right here. This means going to prison - perhaps worse."

"Does it?" he asked, between his set teeth. "If those two brunettes get me, they'll have to go some."

When the two pounced upon him he made no resistance and they captured him. He stood between them, each of them clutching an arm and breathing heavily, not only from exertion, but also out of a sense of triumph.

VI

HE DEPARTS

And now, in order to give a key to the surprising performances of Alexander H. Pike, it will be necessary to call up certain biographical data.

When he was in the Hill School he won the pole vault, but later, in his real collegiate days, he never could come within two inches of 'varsity form, and therefore failed to make the track-team.

While attending the Institute of Technology he worked one whole autumn to perfect an offensive play which was to be used against "Buff" Rodigan, of the semi-professional athletic-club team. This play was known as "giving the shoulder," with the solar plexus as the point of attack. The purpose of the play was not to kill the opposing player, but to induce him to relinquish all interest in the contest.

Furthermore, Mr. Pike, while spending a month or more at a time in New York City, during his post-graduate days, had worked with Mr. Mike Donovan, in order to keep down to weight. Mr. Donovan had illustrated many tricks to him, one of the best being a low feint with the left, followed by a right cross to the point of the jaw.

While the two bronze-colored guards stood holding him, Mr. Pike rapidly took stock of his accomplishments, and formulated a program. With a sudden twist he cleared himself, sprang away from the two, and jumped behind a tree. One soldier started to the right of the tree and the other to the left, so as to close in upon him and retake him. This was what he wanted, for he had them "spread," and could deal with them singly.

He used the Donovan tactics on the first guard, and they worked out with shameful ease. When the soldier saw the left coming for the pit of his stomach, he crouched and hugged himself, thereby extending his jaw so that it waited there with the sun shining on it until the young man's right swing came across and changed the middle of the afternoon to midnight. Number one was lying in profound slumber when Alumnus Pike turned to greet number two.

The second soldier, having witnessed the feat of pugilism, doubled his fists and extended them awkwardly, coming with a rush. Mr. Pike suddenly squatted and leaned forward, balancing on his finger-tips, until number two was about to fall upon him and crush him, and then he arose with that rigid right shoulder aimed as a catapult. There was a sound as when the air-brake is disconnected, and number two curled over limply on the ground and made faces in an effort to resume breathing.

Mr. Pike picked up his magazine and put it under his coat. He buttoned the coat, smiled in a pale, but placid manner at Kalora, who was still immovable with terror, and then he proceeded to vindicate his "prep school" training. He ran over to the canopy tent, under which the refreshments had been served, pulled out one of the poles and, pointing it ahead of him, ran straight for the wall.

Kalora, watching him, regarded this as a wholly insane proceeding. Was he going to attempt to poke a hole through a wall three feet thick?

Just as he seemed ready to flatten himself against the stones, he dropped the end of the pole to the ground and shot upward like a rocket. Kalora saw him give an upward twist and wriggle, fling himself free from the pole and disappear on the other side of the wall, the camera following like the tail of a comet. As he did so, number two, coming to a sitting posture, began to shriek for reinforcements. Number one was up on his elbow, regarding the affairs of this world with a dreamy interest.

Fortunately for the Governor-General, the participants in the exploded garden-party had escaped at the very first opportunity.

Count Malagaski, greatly perturbed and almost in a state of collapse over the unhappy affair in the garden, was returning to his apartments when the second surprising episode of the day came to a noisy climax.

He heard the uproar and had the two guards brought before him. They reported that they had found a stranger in the garb of an infidel seated within the secret garden chatting with the Princess Kalora. They did not agree in their descriptions of him, but each maintained that the intruder was a very large person of forbidding appearance and terrific strength.

"How did he manage to escape?" asked the Governor-General.

"By jumping over the wall."

"Over a wall ten feet high?" demanded the Governor-General.

"Without touching his hands, sir. He was very tall; must have been seven feet."

"If you ever had an atom of gray matter, evidently this stranger has beaten it out of you. Hurry and notify the police!"

Kalora's candid version of the whole affair was hardly less startling than that of the guards. The stranger had come over the wall suddenly, much to her alarm. He attempted to converse with her, but she sternly ordered him from the premises. He was exceedingly tall, as the guards had said, and very dark, with rather long hair and curling black mustache. He addressed her in English, but spoke with a marked German accent.

This description, faithfully set down by Popova, was carried away to the secret police of Morovenia, said to be the most astute in the world. They were instructed to watch all trains and guard the frontier and, as soon as they had their prisoner safely put away in the lower dungeon of the municipal prison, they were to notify the Governor-General, who would privately pass sentence.

A crime against any member of the ruler's household comes under a separate category and need not be tried in public sessions. For entering a royal harem or addressing a woman of title the sentences range from the bastinado to solitary confinement for life.

No wonder Kalora waited in trembling. Like every other provincial she had much respect for the indigenous constabulary. She did not believe it possible for the pleasing stranger to break through the network that would be woven about him.

Shunning her father and sister, and shunned by them, she waited many sleepless hours in her own apartments for the inevitable news from beyond the walls.

Next morning there came to her a cheering and terrifying message.

VII

THE ONLY KOLDO

Three hours after his pole-vault, Mr. Alexander H. Pike, wearing a dinner-jacket newly ironed by his man-slave, and with a soft hat crushed jauntily down over the right ear, was pacing back and forth in the main corridor of the Hotel de l'Europe waiting for the dread summons to the table d'hote.

He had to admit to himself that his nerves seemed to be about as taut as piano wires. He told himself that possibly he was "up against it," and yet he had stood on the brink of disaster so often during his college career without acquiring vertigo, that the experience of the afternoon was like a joyous renewal of youth.

He had no set program but he had a feeling that if he was to be questioned he would lie entertainingly.

Of one thing he was certain - it would help his case if he made no attempt to hurry across the frontier. He believed in the wisdom of hunting up the authorities whenever the authorities were hunting for him. For instance, in the prep school, after getting the cow into the chapel, he discovered her there and notified the principal and was the only boy who did not fall under suspicion. To assume a childlike innocence and to bluff magnificently, - these had been the twin rules that had saved him so often and would save him now, unless he should be confronted by the princess or the two guards, in which case - he whistled softly.

Suddenly two men came slamming in at the front door and stalked down the avenue of palms. They seemed to be throbbing with the importance of their errand, as they moved toward a little side office, which was the official lair of the manager.

One of the men was elderly and wizened and the other was a detective. Pike knew it as soon as he glanced at the heavy jowls and the broad face and heard the authoritative footfall. He knew, also, that he was not a bona fide detective, but a municipal detective, who is paid a monthly salary and walks stealthily along side streets in citizen's dress, all the time imagining that the people he meets take him to be a merchant or a lawyer. In this he is mistaken, for he resembles nothing except a municipal detective.

If Mr. Pike had known that the officer who accompanied Popova was the celebrated Koldo, chief of the secret service, no doubt the impulse to retreat to his apartment and get behind the bed canopies would have been stronger. He knew, however, that no detective of analytical methods would expect to find the criminal standing at his elbow, so he followed the two over to the office and calmly wedged himself into the conference.

The great Koldo was agitated as he told his story to the manager, who was a polite and sympathetic importation from Switzerland. Popova stood by and corroborated by nodding.

"An outrage of the most dreadful nature has been reported from the palace," said Koldo.

"Dear me!" murmured the manager. "I am so sorry."

"A stranger scaled the wall and entered the forbidden precincts. He addressed himself to the Princess Kalora with most insulting familiarity. Two of the household guards captured him, but he escaped after beating them brutally. The report of the whole affair and a description of the man have been brought to me by the esteemed Popova - this gentleman here, who is court interpreter and instructor in languages to the royal family."

Popova nodded and Mr. Pike saw the scattered spires of Bessemer, Pennsylvania, whirling away into a cloud of disappearance.

"If you have a description of the man, no doubt you will be able to find him," he said, knowing that this kind of speech would strengthen his plea of innocence when brought out at the trial.

The chief of the secret service turned and looked wonderingly at the bland stranger and resumed: "After some reflection I have decided to make inquiries at all the hotels, to learn if any foreigner answering this description has lately arrived in the city."

"You may be sure that any information I possess will be put at your disposal immediately," said the manager, with a smile and a professional bow.

The only Koldo, breathing deeply, brought from his pocket a sheet of paper, while Mr. Pike propped himself deliberately against the door and tried to mold his features into that expression of guileless innocence which he had observed on the face of a cherub in the Vatican.

"He is very rugged and powerful," said the detective, referring to his notes. "Large, quite large - black hair, dark eyes with a glance that seems to pierce through anything - long mustache, also black - wears much jewelry - speaks with a marked German accent - wears a suit of Scotch plaid - heavy military boots."

Mr. Pike removed his hat and allowed the electric light to twinkle on his ruddy hair.

"How - ah - where did you get this description?" he asked gently.

"From the Princess herself," replied Popova. "She saw him at close range."

"Believe me, I am sorry, but no one answering the description has been at my hotel," said the manager.

"Then I shall go to the Hotel Bristol and the Hotel Victoria," announced Koldo, with something of fierce determination in his tone.

"An excellent plan," assented the manager.

"Would you mind if I butted in with a suggestion?" said Mr. Pike, laying a friendly hand on the arm of the redoubtable Koldo. "Don't you think it would be better if you went alone to these hotels? This distinguished gentleman," indicating Popova, "is well known on account of being a high guy up at the palace. Sure as you live, if he trails around with you, you will be spotted. You don't want to hunt this fellow with a brass band. Besides, you don't need any help, do you?" - to the head of the secret service.

"Certainly not," replied the famous detective, swelling visibly. "I have all the data - already I am planning my campaign."

"Then I should like to have a talk with Pop-what's-his-name. I think I can slip him a few valuable pointers. You go right along and nail your man and we'll sit here in the shade of the sheltering palm and tell each other our troubles."

"I must return to the palace quite soon," murmured Popova, gazing at the stranger uneasily.

"Call a carriage for the professor," spoke up Mr. Pike briskly, to the manager. "I know his time is valuable, so we'll get down to business immediately, if not sooner."

The manager knew a millionaire's voice when he heard it, so he hurried away. The impatient Koldo said that he would communicate directly with the palace as soon as he had effected the capture, and started for the front door. Then, remembering himself, he went out the back way.

The old tutor, finding himself alone with Mr. Pike, was not permitted to relapse into embarrassment.

"In the first place, I want you to know who and what I am," said Mr. Pike. "Come into my suite and I'll show you something. Then you'll see that you're not wasting your time on a light-weight."

He led the way to a large parlor ornately done in red, and pulled out from a leather trunk a passport issued by the Department of State of the United States of America. It was a huge parchment, with pictorial embellishments, heavy Gothic type and a seal about the size of a pie. Mr. Pike's physical peculiarities were enumerated and there was a direct request that the bearer be shown every courtesy and attention due a citizen of the great republic. Popova looked it over and was impressed.

"It isn't everybody that gets those," said Mr. Pike, as he put the document carefully back into the trunk and covered it with shirts. "Have a red chair. Take off your hat - ah, I remember, you leave that on, don't you?"

The old gentleman seated himself, somewhat reassured by the cheery manner of his host, who sat in front of him and beamed.

Mr. Pike, supposed to be given to vapory and aimless conversation, really was a general. Already we have learned that he based his every-day conduct on a groundwork of safe principles. He had certain private theories, which had stood the test, and when following these theories he proceeded with bustling confidence. One of his theories was that every man in the world has a grievance and regards himself as much-abused, and in order to win the regard and confidence of that man, all one has to do is feel around for the grievance and then play upon it. Mr. Pike, in his province of employer, had been compelled to study the methods of successful labor-union agitators.

George Ade

"You don't know much about me, but I know plenty about you," he began, closing one eye and nodding wisely. "I hadn't been here very long before I found out who was the real brains of that outfit up at the palace."

"Really, you know, we are not supposed to discuss the merits of our ruler," said Popova, fairly startled at the candid tone of the other. He lifted one hand in timid deprecation.

"Of course you're not. That's why some one who is simply a figurehead goes on taking all the credit for tricks turned by a smart fellow who is working for him. Now, if you lived in the dear old land of ready money, where the accident of birth doesn't give any man the right to sit on somebody else's neck, you'd be a big gun. You'd have money and a pull and probably, before you got through, you'd be investigated. Over here, you are deliberately kept in the background. You are the Patsy."

"The what?"

"The squidge - that means the fellow who does all the worrying and gets nothing out of it. Now, before you return to what you call the palace, and which looks to me like the main building of the Allegheny Brick Works, will you do me the honor of going into that cave of gloom, known as the American bar, and hitting up just one small libation?"

"I am not sure that I catch your meaning," said Popova, who felt himself somewhat smothered by rhetoric.

"Into the bar - down at the little iron table - business of hoisting beverage."

"We of the faith are not supposed to partake of any drink containing even a small percentage of alcohol."

"I'm not *supposed* to dally with it myself, having been brought up on cistern water, but I find in traveling that I entertain a more kindly feeling for you strange foreign people when I carry a medium-sized headlight. Come along, now. Don't compel me to tear your clothes."

There was no resisting the masterful spirit of the young steel magnate, and Popova was led away to a remote apartment, where a single shelf, sparsely set with bottles, made a weak effort to reproduce the fabled splendors of far-away New York.

"Let's see, what shall we tackle?" asked Mr. Pike, as he checked down the line with a rigid forefinger. "If you don't care what happens to you, we might try a couple of cocktails - that is, if you like the taste of *eau de quinine*. Oh, I'll tell you what! Here are lemons, seltzer and gin. Boy, two gin fizzes."

The attendant, who was very juvenile and much afraid of his job, smiled and shook his head.

"Do you mean to say that you never heard of a gin fizz?" asked Mr. Pike. "All the ingredients within reach, simply waiting to be introduced to each other, and you have been holding them apart. You ought to be ashamed of yourself. Bring out some ice. Produce your jigger. Get busy. Hand me the tools and I'll do this myself."

Then, while the other two looked on in abashed admiration, Mr. Pike deftly squeezed the lemons and splashed in allopathic portions of the crystal fluid and used ice most wastefully. After vigorous shaking and patient straining he shot a seething stream of seltzer into each glass and finally delivered to Popova a translucent drink that was very tall and capped with foam.

"Hide that, Professor," he said. "In a few minutes you will speak several new languages."

Popova sipped conservatively.

"Don't be afraid," urged Mr. Pike, encouragingly. "If the boy watched me carefully, possibly he can duplicate the order."

The youth was more than willing, for he seldom received instruction. With now and then a word of counsel or warning from the wise man of the west in the corner, he cautiously assembled two other fizzes, while Mr. Pike, in a most nonchalant and roundabout manner, sought information concerning affairs of state, local politics, the Governor-General's household and Princess Kalora. Popova told more than he had meant to tell and more than he knew that he was telling.

It may have been that the fizzes were insidious or that Mr. Pike was unduly persuasive, or that a combination of these two powerful influences moved the elderly tutor to impulses of unusual generosity. At any rate, he found himself possessed of an affection for the young man from Bessemer, Pennsylvania. It was an affection both fatherly and brotherly. When Mr. Pike asked him to perform just a small service for him, he promised and then promised again and was still promising when his host went with him to the carriage and said that he had not lived in vain and that in years to come he would gather his grandchildren around him and tell of the circumstances of his meeting with the greatest scholar in southeastern Europe.

VIII

BY MESSENGER

On the morning after the strange happenings in the garden, Kalora sat by one of the cross-barred windows overlooking a side street, and envied the humble citizens and unimportant woman drifting happily across her field of vision.

Never in all her life had she walked out alone. The sweet privilege of courting adventure had been denied her. And yet she felt, on this morning, an almost intimate acquaintance with the outside world, for had she not talked with a valorous young man who could leap over high walls and subdue giants and pay compliments? He had thrown a sudden glare of romance across her lonesome pathway. The few minutes with him seemed to encompass everything in life that was worth remembering. She told herself that already she liked him better than any other young man she had met, which was not surprising, for he had been the first to sit beside her and look into her eyes and tell her that she was beautiful. She knew that whatever of wretchedness the years might hold in store for her, no local edict could rob her of one precious memory. She had locked it up and put it away, beyond the reach of courts and relatives.

During many wakeful hours she had recalled each minute detail of that amazing interview in the garden, and had tried to estimate and foreshadow the young man's plan of escape from the secret police.

Perhaps he had been taken during the night. The greatest good fortune that she could picture for him was a quick flight across the frontier, which meant that he would never return - that she had seen him once and could not hope to see him again.

In her contemplation of the luminous figure of the Only Young Man, she had ceased to speculate concerning her own misfortunes. The fact of her disgrace remained in the background, eclipsed - not in evidence except as a dim shadow over the day.

While she sat immovable, gazing into the street, feeling within herself a tumult which was not of pain, nor yet of pleasure, but a satisfactory commingling of both, she heard her name spoken. Popova was standing in the doorway. He greeted her with a smile and bow, both of which struck her as being singularly affected, for he was not given to polite observances. As he squatted near her, she noticed that he was tremulous and seemed almost frightened about something.

"I have come to tell you that I regret exceedingly the - the distressing incident of yesterday, and that I sympathize with you deeply - deeply," he began.

"It is your fault," she said, turning from him and again gazing into the street. "You taught me everything I do not need in Morovenia. You neglected the one essential. I am not blind. It was never your desire that I should be like my sister."

She spoke in a low monotone and with no tinge of resentment, but her words had an immediate and perturbing effect on Popova, who stared at her wide-eyed and seemed unable to find his voice.

"You must know that I have been governed by your father's wishes," he said awkwardly. "Why do you - "

"Do not misunderstand me. I thank you for what you have done. I would not be other than what I am. Tell me - the stranger - you know, the one in the garden - has he been taken?" inquired the Princess.

"Taken! Taken! Not even a clue - not a trace! Either the earth opened to swallow him or else Koldo is a dunce. The description was most accurate. By the way, I - I had a most interesting conversation regarding the case, with a young man at the Hotel de l'Europe last evening. He is a person of great importance in his own country, also a student of world-politics - I - he - never have I encountered such discrimination in one so young. It was because of my admiration for his talents and my confidence in his integrity that I consented to deliver a message for him."

Kalora squirmed in her pillows, and turned eagerly to face Popova.

"A message? For me?" she cried, eagerly.

"I will admit that the whole proceeding is most irregular, to put it mildly. The young man was so deeply interested in your perilous adventure of yesterday, and so desirous of felicitating you upon your escape, that I yielded to his importunities and promised to deliver to you this letter."

He brought it out cautiously, as if it were loaded with an explosive, and Kalora pounced upon it.

"I rely upon you to maintain absolute secrecy in regard to my part in this unusual -"

But Kalora, unheeding him, had torn open the letter and was reading, as follows:

MY DEAR PRINCESS:

I hope that's the way to begin. Something tells me that you would not stand for "Your Majesty" or any of these "Royal Highness" trimmings.

Believe me, you are the best ever. I have just had a talk with the eminent plain-clothes man who is looking for the burglar that broke into the garden this afternoon and tried to steal you. He read to me the description. Say, if I tried to write at this minute all of my present emotions concerning you, I would burn holes in the paper. When it comes to turning out fiction, Marie Corelli is not in the running. Honestly, when Mr. Detective walked into the hotel this evening, I figured it a toss-up whether I should ever see home and mother again.

I am only an humble steel-maker, but I am for you and I want to see you again and tell you right to your face what I think of you. If you will sort of happen to be in the garden at 4 p.m. to-morrow (Thursday), I will come over the wall at the very spot I picked out to-day. I know that this method of becoming acquainted with young women is not indorsed by the *Ladies' ome Journal* or Beatrice Fairfax, but, as nearly as I can find out, there is no other way in which I can get into society over here.

So far as the bloodhounds of the law are concerned, don't give them a thought. I have met, the great Koldo, and he won't know until about next Sunday that yesterday was Tuesday. The professor has promised to bring a reply to the hotel. He is not on.

Sincerely,

YOUR GERMAN FRIEND.

She read it all and found herself gasping - surprised, frightened, and moved to a fluttering delight. She had thought of him as skulking in byways, of concealing his name and attempting to disguise himself so that he might dodge through the meshes woven by the invincible Koldo, and here he was, still flaunting himself at the hotel and calmly preparing to repeat his hazardous experiment.

"He is a fool!" she exclaimed, forgetting that Popova was present.

"I trust the message has not offended you," said the tutor, decidedly alarmed at her agitation and not understanding what it meant.

"I tell you he is a fool - a fool!" she repeated. And while Popova wondered, she sprang to her feet and ran to him and gave him a muscular embrace around the tender portion of his neck, for he still squatted after the oriental manner, even though he wore a long black coat of German make.

"I consented to bring it because he was most urgent, and seemed a proper sort of person," began Popova, "and not knowing the contents -"

"Bless you, I am not offended," interrupted Kalora, and then, looking at the letter again, she burst into happy laughter.

The young stranger was unquestionably a fool. She had not dreamed that any one could be so reckless and heedless, so contemptuous of the dread machinery of the law, so willing to risk his very life for the sake of - of seeing her again!

"If he has been impertinent, possibly you will take no notice of his communication," suggested Popova.

"Oh, I *must* - I must at least acknowledge the receipt of it. Common courtesy demands that. I shall write just a few lines and you must take them to him at once. He seems to be a very forward person unacquainted with our local customs, and so I shall formally thank him and suggest to him that any further correspondence would be inadvisable. That's the really proper thing to do, don't you think?"

"Possibly."

"Then wait here until I have written it, and unless you wish me to go to my father and tell him something that would put an end to your illustrious career, deliver this message within a hour - deliver it yourself. Give it to him and to no one else."

Never was a go-between more nonplussed, but he promised with a readiness and a sincerity which indicated that he was keenly aware of the fact that Kalora held him in her power. The minx had read his secret without an effort!

Mr. Pike was waiting in the avenue of potted palms when the greatest scholar of southeastern Europe, now reduced to the humble role of messenger boy, came to him, somewhat flurried and breathless, and slipped a small envelope into his hand.

Popova rather curtly refused to renew his acquaintance with occidental fizzes, and waited only until he had announced to Mr. Pike that the Princess wished to emphasize the advice contained in the letter and to assure the presumptuous stranger that it was meant for his welfare.

This is what Mr. Pike read:

My very good friend:

I have protected you, not because you deserve protection, but because I like you very much. You must not come to the palace grounds again. They are now under double guard and, if I attempted to meet you, no doubt a whole company of our big soldiers would surround you and surely you could not overcome so many powerful men. I am thinking only of your safety. I beg you to leave Morovenia at once. Your danger is greater than you can imagine. What more can I say, except that I shall always remember you? Sincerely,

K.

Mr. Pike read it carefully three times and then told

himself aloud that it was not what he would precisely term a love-letter.

"I may have made an impression, but certainly not a ten-strike," he thought to himself, as he folded up the missive and put it into the most sacred compartment of his Russia-leather pocketbook, along with the letter of credit.

"I fear me that the incident is closed," he said. "I would stay here one year if I thought there was a chance of seeing her again, but if she wants me to fly I guess I had better fly."

That evening, after an earnest controversy with the manager over a very complicated bill, studded with "extras," Mr. Alexander H. Pike, accompanied by dragoman, leather trunks, hat-boxes and hold-alls, drove away to the transcontinenta express, and slept soundly while crossing the dangerous frontier.

Possibly he would not have slept so soundly if he had known that at four o'clock that afternoon the Princess Kalora had been idling her time in the palace garden, walking back and forth near the high wall.

She had told him not to come, and of course he would not come. No one could be so audacious and foolhardy as to invite destruction after being solemnly warned - and yet, if he *did* come, she wanted to be there to speak to him again and rebuke him and tell him not to come a third time.

She went back to her apartment much relieved and intensely disappointed.

Such is the perverseness of the feminine nature, even in Morovenia.

IX

AS TO WASHINGTON, D.C.

About the time that Mr. Pike arrived in Vienna, and after Kalora had been in voluntary retirement for some forty-eight hours, the famous Koldo, head of the secret police, came into possession of a most important clue.

Having searched for two days, without finding the trail of the criminal with the black mustache and the German accent, he bethought himself of the wisdom of going to the garden where the intruder had engaged in a desperate struggle with the two guards. Possibly he would discover incriminating footprints. Instead, he found some scraps of paper, with printing of a foreign character.

By questioning the guards he learned that these tatters had come from a printed book which the mysterious stranger had carried, and which he never relinquished even while reducing his foes to insensibility.

Koldo put these pieces of paper into a strong envelope, which he sealed and marked "Exhibit A," and delivered his precious find to the Governor-General.

While Mr. Pike sat in Ronacher's at Vienna, watching a most entertaining vaudeville performance, Count

Selim Malagaski was in his library, conferring with the wise Popova.

"How did he escape?" asked Count Malagaski again and again, shaking his head. "The police have searched every corner of the town, and can find no one answering the description."

"Have you questioned Kalora again?"

"Yes, and she now remembers that he had a very heavy scar over his right eye. Her description and these few scraps of paper torn from the book he was carrying are all that we have to guide us in our search."

The Governor-General held up the several remnants of a ten-cent magazine.

"It is in English; I read it badly."

He gave the torn pages to the old tutor, and Popova, picking up the first, read as follows:

What is the great danger that threatens the American woman? It is *obesity*. It is well known that ninety-nine per cent of all the women in the United States are striving to reduce their weight. For all such we have a message of hope. Write to Madam Clarissa and she -

"The remainder is torn away," said Popova.

The Governor-General had been leaning forward, listening intently. "Do you mean to say that there is a country in which all the woman are fat?" he asked.

"It would seem so," replied Popova. "Let us read further." He picked up another of the torn pages and read aloud:

To the Oatena Company of Pine Creek, Michigan:

When I began using your wonderful health-food I was a mere skeleton. I have been living on it for three months and I have gained a pound a day. Permit me to express the conviction that you are real benefactors to the human race. Gratefully yours,

OSCAR TILBURY,
Oakdale, Arkansas.

"Stop!" exclaimed the Governor-General, striking the table. "Is it possible that somewhere in this world there is a food which will add a pound a day?"

"The testimonial seems genuine," replied Popova. "It has been sworn to before a notary."

"What country is this?"

"America, the land of milk and honey."

"Both very fattening," commented the Governor-General. "Popova, I have an inspiration. You well know that my situation here is most desperate. I must find husbands for these two daughters, but I dare not hope that any one will come for Kalora until the disgraceful affair has been forgotten and I can absolutely demonstrate that she has developed into some degree of attractiveness. It is better for all concerned that she should leave Morovenia until the present scandal blows over. Now, why not America? It is a remote, half-savage country, and she will be far from the temptations which would beset her at any fashionable capital in Europe. We read in this magazine that all the women in America are fat. She will come back to us in a little while as plump as a partridge. From the sworn testimonial it would appear that she can obtain in America a marvelous food which will cause her to gain a pound a day. She now weighs one hundred and eighteen pounds. If she remained there a year she would weigh, let me see - one hundred and eighteen plus three hundred and sixty-five - oh, that doesn't seem possible! That is too good to be true! But even six months, or only three months, would be sufficient. She *must* be sent away for a while, in the care of some one who will guard her carefully. Read up on America to-night, and let me know all about it in the morning."

Next day Popova, having consulted all the British authorities at hand, reported that the United States of America covered a large but undeveloped area, that the population was so engrossed with the accumulation of wealth that it gave little heed to pleasures or intellectual relaxation, and that the country as a whole was unworthy of consideration except as the abode of a swollen material prosperity.

"Just the place for her," exclaimed the Governor-General. "No pleasures to distract her, an atmosphere of plodding commercialism, an abundance of health-giving nourishment! Perhaps the mere change of climate will have the desired effect. We will make the experiment. She is doomed if she remains here, and America seems to be our only hope. I suppose our beloved Monarch sends a minister to that country. If so, communicate with the Secretary of the Legation and request him to secure secluded apartments for her and a suite. You shall accompany her."

"I?" exclaimed Popova, unable to conceal his joy.

"Yes; she must be under careful restraint all the time. What is the capital of the United States?"

"Washington. It is a sleepy and well-behaved town. I have looked it up."

"Good! You shall take her to Washington. If one of the many civil wars should break out, or there should be an uprising of the red men, she can hurry to the protection of the Turkish Embassy. Let us make immediate preparations - and remember, Popova, that my whole future happiness as a father depends upon the success of this expedition."

When Kalora was gravely informed by her father that she and the tutor and a half-dozen female attendants were to be bundled up and sent away to America, and that she was to do penance, take a dieting treatment, and come back in due time to try and atone for her unfortunate past, did she weep and beg to be allowed to remain at her own dear home? No; she listened in apparently meek and rather mournful submission, and, after her father went away, she turned handsprings across the room.

Her utmost dream of happiness had been realized. She was to go to the land of the red-headed stranger where she would be admired and courted, and where, in time, she might aspire to the ultimate honor of having her picture in a ten-cent magazine.

X

ON THE WING

The train rolled away from the low and dingy station and was in the open country of Morovenia. Kalora and her elderly guardian and the young women who were to be her companions during the period of exile had been tucked away into adjoining compartments. Each young woman was muffled and veiled according to the most discreet and orthodox rules.

Popova's bright red fez contrasted strangely with his silvering hair, but no more strangely than did this wondrous experience of starting for a new world contrast with the quiet years that he had spent among his books.

The train sped into the farm-lands. On either side was a wide stretch of harvest fields, heaving into gentle billows, with here and there a shabby cluster of buildings. If Kalora had only known, Morovenia was very much like the far-away America, except that Morovenia had not learned to decorate the hillsides with billboards.

At last she was to have a taste of freedom! No father to scold and plead; no much-superior sister to torment her with reproaches; no peering through grated windows at one little rectangle of outside sunshine. To be sure, Popova had received explicit and positive instructions concerning her government. But Popova - pshaw!

She unwound her veil and removed her head-gear and sat bareheaded by the car-window, greedily welcoming each new picture that swung into view.

"You must keep your face covered while we are in public or semi-public places," said Popova gently, repeating his instructions to the very letter.

"I shall not."

Thus ended any exercise of Popova's authority during the whole journey.

Before the train had come to Budapest all the young women, urged on to insubordination, had removed their veils, and Kalora had boldly invaded another compartment to engage in rapt and feverish dialogue with a little but vivacious Frenchwoman.

Two hours out from Vienna, the tutor found her involved in a business conference with a guard of the train. She had learned that the tickets permitted a stopover in Vienna. She wished to see Vienna. She had decided to spend one whole day in Vienna.

Popova, as usual, made a feeble show of maintaining his authority, but he was overruled.

Count Selim Malagaski, at home, consulting the prearranged schedule, said, "This morning they have arrived in Paris and Popova is arranging for the steamship tickets."

At which very moment, Kalora was in an open carriage driving from one Vienna shop to another, trying to find ready-made garments similar to those worn by Mrs. Rawley Plumston. Popova was now a bundle-carrier.

The shopping in Vienna was merely a prelude to a riotous extravagance of time and money in Paris. Popova, writing under dictation, sent a message to Morovenia to the effect that they had been compelled to wait a week in order to get comfortable rooms on a steamer.

Kalora had the dressmakers working night and day.

She and her mother and her grandmother and her great-grandmother and the whole line of maternal ancestors had been under suppression and had attired themselves according to the directions of a religious Prophet, who had been ignorant concerning color effects. And yet, now that Kalora had escaped from the cage, the original instinct asserted itself. The love of finery can not be eliminated from any feminine species.

When she boarded the steamer she was outwardly a creature of the New World.

From the moment of embarking she seemed exhilarated by the salt air and the spirit of democracy.

She lingered in New York - more shopping.

By the time she arrived at Washington and went breezing in to call upon a certain dignified young Secretary, the transformation was complete. She might not have been put together strictly according to mode, but she was learning rapidly, and willing to learn more rapidly.

XI

AN OUTING - A REUNION

The Secretary of the Legation at Washington was surprised to receive a letter from the Governor-General of Morovenia requesting him to find apartments for the Princess Kalora and a small retinue. The letter explained that the Governor-General's daughter had been given a long sea-voyage and assigned to a period of residence within the quiet boundaries of Washington, in the hope that her health might be improved.

The Secretary looked up the list of hotels and boarding-houses. He did not deem it advisable to send a convalescent to one of the large and busy hotels; neither did he think it proper to reserve rooms for her at an ordinary boarding-house, where she would sit at the same table with department-employees and congressmen. So he compromised on a very exclusive hotel patronized by legislators who had money of their own, by many of the titled attaches of the embassies, and by families that came during the season with the hope of edging their way into official society. He explained to the manager of the hotel that the Princess Kalora was an invalid, would require secluded apartments, and probably would not care to meet any of the other persons living at the hotel.

Within a week after the rooms had been reserved the invalid drove up to the Legation to thank the Secretary for his kindness. Now, the Secretary had lived in modern capitals for many years, was trained in diplomacy, and had schooled himself never to appear surprised. But the Princess Kalora fairly bowled him over. He had pictured her as a wan and waxen creature, who would be carried to the hotel in a closed carriage or ambulance, there to recline by the windowside and look out at the rustling leaves. He had decided, after hours of deliberation, that the etiquette of the situation would be for some member of the Legation to call upon her about once a week and take flowers to her.

And here was the invalid, bounding out of a coupé, tripping up the front steps and bursting in upon him like an untamed Amazon from the prairies of Nebraska. She wore a tailor-made suit of dark material, a sailor hat, tan gloves with big welts on the back and stout, low-heeled Oxfords. This was the young woman who had come five thousand miles to improve her health! This was the child of the Orient, and in the Orient, woman is a hothouse flower. This was the timid young recluse to whom the soft-spoken diplomats were to carry a few roses about once a week.

Why had she called upon the Secretary? First, to thank him for having engaged the rooms; second, to invite him to take her out to a country club and teach her the game of golf. She had heard people at the hotel talking about golf. The game had been strongly commended to her by a congressman's daughter, with whom she had ascended to the top of the Washington Monument.

When the Secretary, having recovered his breath, asked if she felt strong enough to attempt such a vigorous game, she was moved to silvery laughter. She told what she had accomplished during three short days in Washington. She had attended two matinees with Popova, had gone motoring into the Virginia hills, had inspected all the public buildings, and studied every shop-window in Pennsylvania Avenue. The Secretary knew that all this outdoor freedom was not usually accorded a young woman of his native domain, and yet he felt that he had no authority to restrain her or correct her. She was a princess, and he was relatively a subordinate, and, when she requested him to take her to the country club, he gave an embarrassed consent.

"You have been in America a long time?" she asked.

"About three years."

"You have met many people - that is, the important people?"

"All of them are important over here. Those that are not very wealthy or very eminent are getting ready to be."

"I am wondering if you could tell me something about a young man I met abroad. I met him only once, and I have quite forgotten his name."

"I'm afraid I haven't met him."

"He is rather good-looking and has - well, red hair; not rusty red, but a sort of golden red."

"There are millions of red-haired young men in America."

"Please don't discourage me. Now I remember the name of his home. He lived in Pennsa - Pennsylvania, that's it."

"Pennsylvania is about four times as large as Morovenia."

"But he is very wealthy. He talked as if he had come into millions."

"I can well believe it. The millionaires of Pennsylvania are even as the sands of the sea or the leaves of the forest."

"He owns some sort of mills or factories - where they make steel."

"Every millionaire in Pennsylvania has something to do with steel. Now, if you were searching in that state for a young man who is penniless and has nothing to do with the steel industry, possibly I might be of some service to you. The whole area of Pennsylvania is simply infested with millionaires. Not all of them are red-headed, but they will be, before Congress gets through with them."

This playful lapse into the American vernacular was quite lost upon the Princess Kalora, who was sitting very still and gazing in a most disconsolate manner at the Secretary.

"I felt sure that you could tell me all about him," she said.

"Believe me, if I encounter any young millionaire from Pennsylvania, whose hair is golden-red, I shall put detectives on his trail and let you know at once. You met him abroad?"

"At a garden party in Morovenia."

"Indeed! Garden parties in Morovenia! And yet that is not one-half as surprising as to find you here in Washington."

"You are not displeased to find me here?"

"Charmed - delighted."

"And you will take me to the country club?"

"At any time. It will really give me much pleasure."

"I shall drop a note. Good-by."

He stood at the window to watch her as she nimbly jumped into the coupé and was driven away.

That evening he made a most astonishing report to his intimates of the corps and asked:

"What shall I do?"

"Do you feel competent to take charge of her and regulate her conduct?"

"I do not."

"Have you instructions to watch her and make sure that she observes the etiquette and keeps within the restrictions of her own country while she is visiting in Washington?"

"Nothing of the sort."

"From your first interview with her, do you believe that it would be advisable for any of us to attempt to interfere with her plans?"

"Decidedly not."

"Then take her to the country club and teach her the game of golf, and remember the old saying at home, that no man was ever given praise for attempting to govern another man's family."

So it was settled that the Legation would not attempt any supervision of Kalora's daily program. And it was a very wise decision, for the daily program was complicated and the Legation would have been kept exceedingly busy.

Popova became merely a sort of footman, or modified chaperon. He knew that he had no real authority and seldom attempted even the most timid suggestions as to her conduct. Once or twice he mentioned health-food and dieting, and was pooh-poohed into a corner. As for the women attendants, who had been sent along that they might be the companions of the Princess during the long hours of loneliness and seclusion, they were trained to act as hair-dressers and French maids and repairing seamstresses!

Kalora had money and a title and physical attractions. Could she well escape the gaieties of Washington? Be assured that she made no effort to escape them. She followed the busy routine of dinners and balls, receptions and afternoon teas, her childish enthusiasm never lagging. She could play at golf and she seemed to know horseback riding the first time she tried it, and after the first two weeks she drove her own motor-car.

The letters that went back to Morovenia were fairly dripping with superlatives and happy adjectives. She was delighted with Washington; she was in excellent health; the members of the Legation were very thoughtful in their attentions; the autumn weather was all that could be desired; her apartments at the hotel were charming. In fact, her whole life was rose-colored, but never a word of real news for her anxious father and sister - nothing about gaining a pound a day. The Governor-General hoped from the encouraging tone of the letters that she was quietly housed, out in the borders of some primeval forest, gradually enlarging into the fullness of perfect womanhood.

About three months after her departure, in order to reassure himself regarding the progress in her case, he wrote a letter to the minister at Washington. He told the minister that his child was disposed to be unruly and that Popova had become careless and somewhat indefinite in his reports - and would he, the minister, please write and let an anxious parent know the actual weight of Princess Kalora?

The minister resented this manner of request. He did not feel that it was within the duties of a high official to go out and weigh young women, so he replied briefly that he knew no way of ascertaining the exact weight of an acrobatic young woman who never stood still long enough to be weighed, but he could assure the father that she was somewhat slimmer and more petite than when she arrived in Washington a few weeks before.

This letter slowly traveled back to Morovenia, and on the very day of its delivery to Count Selim Malagaski, who read it aloud and then went into a frothing paroxysm of rage, the Princess Kalora in Washington figured in a most joyful episode.

A western millionaire, who had bought a large cubical palace on one of the radiating avenues, was giving a dancing-party, to which the entire blue book had been invited. Kalora went, trailed by the long-suffering Popova. She wore her most fetching Parisian gown, and decked herself out with wrought jewelry of quaint and heavy design, which was the envy of all the other young women in town, and she put in a very busy night, for she danced with army officers, and lieutenants of the navy, and one senator, and goodness knows how many half-grown diplomats.

At two o'clock in the morning she was in the supper-room: a fairly late hour for a young woman supposed to be leading a quiet life. The food set before her would not have been prescribed for a tender young creature who was dieting. She was supping riotously on stuffed olives. Her companion was a young gentleman from the army. They sat beneath a huge palm. The tables were crowded together rather closely.

She chanced to look across at the little table to her right, and she saw a young man - a young man with light hair almost ripe enough to be auburn.

With a smothered "Oh!" she dropped the olive poised between her fingers, and as she did so, he looked across and saw her and exclaimed:

"Well, I'll be -"

He came over, almost upsetting two tables in his impetuous course. She expected to see him jump over them.

He seized her hand and gazed at her in grinning delight, and the young gentleman from the army went into total eclipse.

XII

THE GOVERNOR CABLES

"I don't believe it. It's too good to be true. I am in a trance. It isn't you, is it?"

And he was still holding her hand.

"Yes - it is."

"The Princess - ah -?"

"Kalora."

"*That's* it. I was so busy thinking of you after I left your cute little country that I couldn't remember the name. I thought of 'calico' and 'Fedora' and 'Kokomo' and a lot of names that sounded like it, but I knew I was wrong. *Kalora - Kalora -* I'll remember that. I knew it began with a 'K.' But what in the name of all that is pure and sanctified are you doing in the land of the free?"

"You invited me to come. Don't you remember? You urged me to come."

"That's why you notified me as soon as you arrived, isn't it? How long have you been here?"

George Ade

"I forget - three months - four months. Surely you have seen my name in the papers. Every morning you may read a full description of what Princess Kalora of Morovenia wore the night before. For a simple and democratic people you are rather fond of high-sounding titles, don't you think?"

"I haven't read the papers, because I'm always afraid I'll find something about myself. They don't describe my costumes, however. They simply say that I am trying to blow up and scuttle the ship of State. But this has nothing to do with your case. It is customary, when you accept an invitation, to let the host know something about it. In other words, why didn't you drop me a line?"

"I will confess - the whole truth - since you have been candid enough to admit that you had forgotten my name. I tried to find you, through the Legation. I described you, but - your name - *please* tell me your name again? You mentioned it, that day in the garden. Popova promised to go to the hotel and get it for me, but we were bundled away in such a hurry."

"Heavens! Imagine any one forgetting such a name! Alexander H. Pike, Bessemer, Pennsylvania, tariff-fed infant and all-round plutocrat."

"Why, of course, *Pike, Pike* - it is the name of a fish."

"Thank you."

The young gentleman from the army moved uneasily, and they remembered that he was present. He hoped they wouldn't mind if he went to look up his partner for the next dance, and they assured him that they wouldn't, and he believed them and was backing away when Popova arrived to suggest the lateness of the hour and intimate his willingness to return to the hotel.

His sudden journey to the western hemisphere and his period of residence at Washington had been punctuated with surprises, but the amazement which smote him when he saw Kalora leaning across the table toward the young man who had introduced the gin fizz into Morovenia was sudden and shocking.

Mr. Pike greeted him rapturously and gave him the keys to North America, and then Kalora patted him on the arm and sent him away to wait for her.

They sat and talked for an hour - sat and talked and laughed and pieced out between them the wonderful details of that very lively day in Morovenia.

"And you have come all the way to Washington, D.C. in order to increase your weight?" he asked. "That certainly would make a full-page story for a Sunday paper. Think of anybody's coming to Washington to fatten up! Why, when I come down here to regulate these committees, I lose a pound a day."

"I never dreamed that there could be a country in which women are given so much freedom - so many liberties."

"And what we don't give them, they take - which is eminently correct. Of all the sexes, there is only one that ever made a real impression on me."

"And to think that some day I shall have to return to Morovenia!"

"Forget it," urged Mr. Pike, in a low and soothing tone. "Far be it from me to start anything in your family, but if I were you, I would never go back there to serve a life sentence in one of those lime-kilns, with a curtain over my face. You are now at the spot where woman is real superintendent of the works, and this is where you want to camp for the rest of your life."

"But I can not disobey my father. I dare not remain if he -"

She paused, realizing that the talk had led her to dangerous ground, for Mr. Pike had dropped his large hand on her small one and was gazing at her with large devouring eyes.

"You won't go back if I can help it," he said, leaning still nearer to her. "I know this is a little premature, even for me, but I just want you to know that from the minute I looked down from the wall that day and saw you under the tree - well, I haven't been able to find anything else in the world worth looking at. When I met you again to-night, I didn't remember your name. You didn't remember my name. What of that? We know each other pretty well - don't you think we do? The way you looked at me, when I came across to speak to you - I don't know, but it made me believe, all at once, that maybe you had been thinking of me, the same as I had been thinking of you. If I'm saying more than I have a right to say, head me off, but, for once in my life, I'm in earnest."

"I'm glad - you like me," she said, and she pushed back in her chair and looked down and away from him and felt that her face was burning with blushes.

"When you have found out all about me, I hope you'll keep on speaking to me just the same," he continued. "I warn you that, from now on, I am going to pester you a lot. You'll find me sitting on your front door-step every morning, ready to take orders. To-morrow I must hie me to New York, to explain to some venerable directors why the net earnings have fallen below forty per cent. But when I return, O fair maiden, look out for me."

He would be back in Washington within three days. He would come to her hotel. They were to ride in the motor-car and they were to go to the theaters. She must meet his mother. His mother would take her to New York, and there would be the opera, and this, and that, and so on, for he was going to show her all the attractions of the Western Hemisphere.

The night was thinning into the grayness of dawn when he took her to the waiting carriage. She put her hand through the window and he held it for a long time, while they once more went over their delicious plans.

After the carriage had started, Popova spoke up from his dark corner.

"I am beginning to understand why you wished to come to America. Also I have made a discovery. It was Mr. Pike who overcame the guards and jumped over the wall."

"I shall ask the Governor-General to give you Koldo's position."

An enormous surprise was waiting for them at the hotel. It was a cable from Morovenia - long, decisive, definite, composed with an utter disregard for heavy tolls. It directed Popova to bring the shameless daughter back to Morovenia immediately - not a moment's delay under pain of the most horrible penalties that could be imagined. They were to take the first steamer. They were to come home with all speed. Surely there was no mistaking the fierce intent of the message.

Popova suffered a moral collapse and Kalora went into a fit of weeping. Both of them feared to return and yet, at such a crisis, they knew that they dared not disobey.

The whole morning was given over to hurried packing-up. An afternoon train carried them to New York. A steamer was to sail early next day, and they went aboard that very night.

Kalora had left a brief message at her hotel in Washington. It was addressed to Mr. Alexander H. Pike, and simply said that something dreadful had happened, that she had been called home, that she was going back to a prison the doors of which would never swing open for her, and she must say good-by to him for ever.

She tried to communicate with him before sailing away from New York. Messenger boys, bribed with generous cab-fares, were sent to all the large hotels, but they could not find the right Mr. Pike. The real Mr. Pike was living at a club.

She leaned over the railing and watched the gang-plank until the very moment of sailing, hoping that he might appear. But he did not come, and she went to her state-room and tried to forget him, and to think of something other than the reception awaiting her back in the dismal region known as Morovenia.

George Ade

XIII

THE HOME-COMING

The Governor-General waited in the main reception-room for the truant expedition. He was hoping against hope. Orders had been given that Popova, Kalora and the whole disobedient crew should be brought before him as soon as they arrived. His wrath had not cooled, but somehow his confidence in himself seemed slowly to evaporate, as it came time for him to administer the scolding - the scolding which he had rehearsed over and over in his mind.

He heard the rolling wheels grit on the drive outside, and then there was murmuring conversation in the hallway, and then Kalora entered. His most dreadful suspicions were ten times confirmed. She wore no veil and no flowing gown. She was tightly incased in a gray cloth suit, and there was no mistaking the presence of a corset underneath. On her head was a kind of Alpine hat with a defiant feather standing upright at one side. Before her father had time to study the details of this barbaric costume, he sat staring at her as she was silhouetted for an instant between him and the open window.

Merciful Mahomet! She was as lean and supple as an Austrian race-horse!

He could say nothing. She ran over and gave him a smack on the forehead and then said cheerily:

"Well, popsy, here I am! What do you think of me?"

While Count Selim Malagaski was holding to his chair and trying to sort out from the limited vocabulary of Morovenia the words that could express his boiling emotions, he saw Popova standing shamefaced in the doorway. Was it really Popova? The tutor wore a traveling-suit with large British checks, a blue four-in-hand, and, instead of a fez, a rakish cap with a peak in front. As he edged into the room the young women attendants filed timidly behind him. Horror upon horrors! They were in shirt-waists, with skirts that came tightly about the hips, and every one of them wore a chip hat, and not one of them was veiled!

The Governor-General tried to steady himself in order to meet this unprecedented crisis.

"So this is how you have managed my affairs?" he said in angry tones to the trembling Popova.

"What is the meaning of this shocking exhibition?"

"Don't blame him, father," spoke up Kalora. "I am responsible for whatever has happened. We have seen something of the world. We have learned that Morovenia is about two hundred years behind the times. They knew that you would not approve, but I have compelled them to have the courage of their convictions. You can see for yourself that we no longer belong here. There is but one thing for you to do, and that is to send us away again."

"No!" exclaimed her father, banging his fist on the table, and then coming to his feet. "You shall remain here - all of you - and be punished! You have ruined your own prospects; you have condemned your poor sister to a life of single misery, and you have made your father the laughing-stock of all Morovenia! If I can not reform you and make you a dutiful child, at least I can make an example of you!"

"Stop!" she said very sharply. "Let us not have an unfortunate scene in the presence of the servants. If you have anything to say to me, send them away, and remember also, father, I have certain rights which even you must respect. Also, I have a great surprise for you. I am beautiful. Hundreds of young men have told me so. Under no circumstances would I permit myself to become large and gross and bulky. You are disheartened because no young man in Morovenia wishes to marry me. Bless you, there isn't a young man in this country worth marrying!"

"Young woman, you have taxed my patience far beyond the limit," said her father, speaking low in an effort to control his wrath. "Hereafter you shall never go beyond the walls of this palace! You shall be a waiting-maid for your sister! The servants shall be instructed to treat you as a menial - one of their own class! These shameless women are dismissed from my service! As for you" - turning upon the old tutor - "you shall be put away under lock and key until I can devise some punishment severe enough to fit your case!"

That night Kalora slept on a hard and narrow cot in a bare apartment adjoining her sister's gorgeous boudoir - quite a change from the suite overlooking the avenue.

The shirt-waist brigade had been sent into banishment, and poor Popova was sitting on a wooden stool in a dungeon, thinking of the dinners he had eaten at Old Point Comfort and wondering if he had not overplayed himself in the effort to be avenged upon the Governor-General.

XIV

HEROISM REWARDED

A month later Popova was still in prison, and had demonstrated that even after one has lunched for several months at the Shoreham, the New Willard and the Raleigh, he may subsist on such simple fare as bread and water.

Kalora had been humiliated to the uttermost, but her spirit was unbroken and defiant.

She was nominally a servant, but Jeneka and the others dared not attempt any overbearing attitude toward her, for they feared her sharp and ready wit.

The fires of inward wrath seemed to have reduced her weight a few pounds, so that if ever a man faced a situation of unbroken gloom, that man was the poor Governor-General.

Count Malagaski sat in the large, over-decorated audience room, alone with his sorrowful meditations. An attendant brought him a note.

"The man is at the gate," said the attendant. "He started to come in. We tried to keep him out. He pushed three of the soldiers out of the way, but we finally held him back, so he sends this note."

A few lines had been written in pencil on the reverse side of a typewritten business letter. The Governor-General could speak English, but he read it rather badly, so he sent for his secretary, who told him that the note ran as follows:

You don't know me and there is no need to give my name. Must see you on important matter of business. Something in regard to your daughter.

"Great Heavens, another one!" said the Governor-General. "There are one thousand young men ready and willing to marry Jeneka and not one in all the world wants Kalora. Send him away!"

"I am afraid he won't go," suggested the attendant. "He is a very positive character."

"Then send him in to me. I can dispose of his case in short order."

A few moments later Count Selim Malagaski found himself sitting face to face with a ruddy young man in a blue suit - a square-shouldered, smiling young gentleman, with hair of subdued auburn.

"I take it that you're a busy man and I'll come to the point," said the young man, pulling up his chair. "I try to be business from the word go, even in matters of this kind. You have a daughter."

"I have two daughters," replied the Governor-General sadly.

"You have only one that interests me. I have been around a good deal, but she is about the finest looking girl I -"

"Before you say any more, let me explain to you," said the Governor-General very courteously. "Perhaps you are not entitled to this information, but you seem to be a gentleman and a person of some importance, and you have done me the honor to admire my daughter, and, therefore, it is well that you should know all the facts in the case. I have two daughters. One is exceedingly beautiful and her hand has been sought in marriage by young men of the very first families of Morovenia, notably Count Luis Muldova, who owns a vast estate near the Roumanian frontier. I have another daughter who is decidedly unattractive, so much so that she has never had an offer of marriage. I am telling you all this because it is known to all Morovenia, and even you, a stranger, would have learned it very soon. Under the law here, a younger sister may not marry until the elder sister has married. My unattractive daughter is the elder of the two. Do you see the point? Do you understand, when you come talking of a marriage with my one desirable daughter, that not only are you competing with all the wealthy and titled young men of this country, but also you are condemned to sit down and patiently wait until the elder sister has married, - which means, my dear sir, that probably you will wait for ever? Therefore I think I may safely wish you good day."

"Hold on, here," said the visitor, who had been listening intently, with his eyes half-closed, and nodding his head quickly as he caught the points of the unusual situation. "If I can fix it up with you and daughter - and I don't think I'll have any trouble with daughter - what's the matter with my rustling around and finding a good man for sister? There is no reason why any young woman with a title should go into the discard these days. At least we can make a try. I have tackled propositions that looked a good deal tougher than this."

"Do you think it possible that you could find a desirable husband for a young woman who has no physical charms and who, on two or three occasions, has scandalized our entire court?"

"I don't say I can, but I'm willing to take a whirl at it."

"My dear sir, before we go any further, tell me something about yourself. You are an Englishman, I presume?"

"Great Scott! You're the first one that ever called me that. I have been called a good many things, but never an Englishman. I'll have to begin wearing a flag in my hat. I'm an American."

"American!" gasped the Governor-General. "I am very sorry to hear it. I have every reason for regarding you and your native country as my natural enemies."

"You're dead wrong. America is all right. The States size up pretty well alongside of this little patch of country."

"I do not blame you for being loyal to your own home, sir, but isn't it rather presumptuous for you, an American, to aspire to the hand of a Princess who could marry any one of a dozen young men of wealth and social position?"

"What's the matter with my wealth and social position? I'm willing to stack up my bank-account with any other candidate. I happen to be worth eighteen million dollars."

"Dollars?" repeated the Governor-General, puzzled. "What would that be in piasters?"

"It's a shame to tell you. Only about four hundred million piastres, that's all."

"What!" exclaimed the Governor-General. "Surely you are joking. How could one man be worth four hundred million piasters?"

"Say, if you'll give me a pencil and a pad of paper and about a half-day's time, I'll figure out for you what Henry Frick is worth in piasters and then you *would* have a fit. Why, in the land of ready money I'm only a third-rater, but I've got the four hundred million, all right."

"But have you any social position?" asked the Governor-General. "Any rank? Any title? Over here those things count for a great deal."

"I am Grand Exalted Ruler of the Benevolent and Protective Order of Elks," said the visitor calmly.

"Really!"

"I am a Knight Templar."

"A knight? That is certainly something."

"Do you see this badge with all the jewels in it? That

means that I am a Noble of the Mystic Shrine."

"I can see that it is the insignia of a very distinguished order," said the Governor-General, as he touched it admiringly.

"What is more, I am King of the Hoo-Hoos."

"A king?"

"A sure-enough king. Now, don't you worry about my wealth or my title. I've got money to burn and I can travel in any company. The thing for us to do is to get together and find a good husband for the cripple, and fix up this whole marriage deal. But before we go into it I want to meet your daughter and find out exactly how I stand with her."

"That will be unnecessary, and also impossible. Whatever arrangements you make with me may be regarded as final. My daughter will obey my wishes."

"Not for mine! I am not trying to marry any girl that isn't just as keen for me as I am for her. Why, I've seen her only twice. Let me talk it over with her, and if she says yes, then you can look me up in Bradstreet and we'll all know where we stand."

"I am sorry, but it is absolutely contrary to our customs to permit a private interview between an unmarried woman and her suitor."

"Whereas in our country it is the most customary thing in the world! Now, why should we observe the customs of *your* country and disregard the customs of *my* country, which is about forty times as large and eighty times as important as your country? Don't be foolish! I may be the means of pulling you out of a tight hole. You go and send your daughter here to me. Give me ten minutes with her. I'll state my case to her, straight from the shoulder, and, if she doesn't give me a lot of encouragement, I'll grab the first train back to Paris. If she *does* give me any encouragement, then you'll see what can be accomplished by a real live matrimonial agency."

The Governor-General hesitated, but not for long. The confident manner of the stranger had inspired him with the first courage that he had felt for many weeks and revived in him the long-slumbering hope that possibly there was somewhere in the world a desirable husband for Kalora. He was about to violate an important rule, but there was no reason why any one on the outside should hear about it.

"This is most unusual," he said. "If I comply with your request, I must beg of you not to mention the fact of this interview to any one. Remain here."

He went away, and the young man waited minute after minute, pacing back and forth the length of the room, cutting nervous circles around the big office chairs, wiping his palms with his handkerchief and wondering if he had come on a fool's errand or whether -

He heard a rustle of soft garments, and turned. There in the doorway stood a feminine full moon - an elliptical young woman, with half of her pink and corpulent face showing above a gauzy veil, her two chubby hands clasped in front of her, the whole attitude one of massive shyness.

"I - I beg pardon," he said, staring at her in wonder.

She tried to speak, but was too much flustered. He saw that she was smiling behind the veil, and then she came toward him, holding out her hand. He took the hand, which felt almost squashy, and said:

"I am very glad to meet you."

Then there was a pause.

"Won't you be seated?" he asked.

She sank into one of the leather chairs and looked up at him with a little simper, and there was another pause.

"I - I never have seen you before, have I?" she asked, with a secretive attempt to take a good look at him.

"You can search me," he replied, staring at her, as if fascinated by her wealth of figure. "If I had seen you before, I have a remote suspicion that I should remember you. I don't think it would be easy to forget you."

"You flatter me," she said softly.

"Do I? Well, I meant every word of it. Will you pardon me for being a wee bit personal? Are there many young ladies in these parts that are as - as - corpulent, or fat, or whatever you want to call it - that is, are you any plumper than the average?"

"I have been told that I am."

"Once more pardon me, but have you done anything for it?"

George Ade

"For what?" she asked, considerably surprised.

"I wouldn't have mentioned it, only I think I can give you some good tips. I had a Cousin Flora who was troubled the same way. About the time she went to Smith College she got kind of careless with herself, used to eat a lot of candy and never take any exercise, and she got to be an awful looking thing. If you'll cut out the starchy foods and drink nothing but Kissingen, and begin skipping the rope every day, you'll be surprised how much of that you'll take off in a little while. At first you won't be able to skip more than twenty-five or fifty times a day, but you keep at it and in a month you can do your five hundred. Put on plenty of flannels and wear a sweater. And I'll show you a dandy exercise. Put your heels together this way," - and he stood in front of her, - "and try to touch the floor with your fingers - so!" - illustrating. "You won't be able to do it at first, but keep at it, and it'll help a lot. Then, if you will lie flat on your back every morning, and work your feet up and down -"

She had listened, at first in utter amazement. Now her timid coquettishness was giving way to anger.

"What are you trying to tell me?" she asked.

"It's none of my business, but I thought you'd be glad to find out what'd take off about fifty pounds."

"And is this why you came to see me?" she demanded.

"*I* didn't come to see *you*."

"My father said you were waiting and he sent me to you."

"Sent *you*," replied Mr. Pike in frank surprise. "My dear girl, you may be good to your folks and your heart may be in the right place, and I don't want to hurt your feelings, but father has got mixed in his dates. I certainly didn't come here to see *you*."

As he was speaking Jeneka wriggled forward in her chair and then arose. She stood before him, heaving perceptibly.

"Your manner is most insulting," she declared. She had expected to be showered with compliments, and here was this giggling stranger advising her to be thin! She toddled over to the door and pushed a bell. Then she turned upon the bewildered stranger and remarked coldly: "Unless you have something further to communicate, you may consider this interview at an end."

A servant appeared in the doorway.

"Show this person out," said the portly princess.

The servant gave a little scream.

"Mr. Pike!"

"Kalora!"

And then he was holding both her hands.

"You are *here* - here in Morovenia? You came all the way?"

"All the way! I'd have come ten times as far. Before I left New York I heard about all those messenger boys hunting me around the hotels, but I didn't know what it meant. When I got back to Washington I found your note, and, as soon as I could get Congress calmed down, I started - got in here last night."

"But why did you come?"

"Can't you guess?" Mr. Pike wasted no time in circumlocution.

During this hurried interview Jeneka had been holding a determined thumb against the electric button. The Governor-General, waiting impatiently up the hallway, heard the prolonged buzzing and came to investigate. He found the adorable Jeneka, all trembling with indignation, in the doorway. She saw him and pointed. He looked and saw the distinguished stranger, the man of many titles and unbounded wealth, standing close to the slim princess, holding both her hands and beaming upon her with all of the unmistakable delirious happiness of love's young dream.

"What does it mean?" asked the Governor-General. "Is it possible -"

"He was rude to me," began Jeneka, "He was most insulting -"

Mr. Pike turned to meet his prospective father-in-law.

"You meant well, but you got twisted," he remarked. "This is the one I was looking for."

At first Count Selim Malagaski was too dumfounded for speech.

"Are you sure?" he asked. "Can it be possible that you,

a man worth millions of piasters, an exalted ruler, a Noble of the Mystic Shrine, have deliberately chosen this waspy, weedy -"

"Let up!" said Mr. Pike sharply. "You can say what you please about your daughter, but you mustn't make remarks about the prospective Mrs. Pike. I don't know anything about her local reputation for looks, but I think she's the most beautiful thing that ever drew breath, and I'd make it stronger than that if I knew how. You thought I meant the fat one. Well, I didn't, but I hope the agreement goes just the same. And I'll stick to what I said. I'll get the other one married off. It may take a little time, but I think I can find some one."

"*Find* some one?" cried Jeneka indignantly.

"*Find* some one?" repeated her father. "She has been sought by every young man of quality in the whole kingdom. How dare you suggest that -"

Then he paused, for he was beginning to comprehend that young Mr. Pike had stepped in and saved him, and that, instead of rebuking Mr. Pike, he should be weeping on his breast and calling him "son."

Jeneka came to her senses at the same moment, for she saw her dream of five years coming true. She knew that soon she would be the Countess Muldova.

Mr. Pike suddenly felt himself caressed by three happy mortals.

"I shall make you a Knight of the Gleaming Scimitar," said the Governor-General. "I have the authority."

"Thanks," replied Mr. Pike.

"And we can have a double wedding," exclaimed Jeneka, whose ecstasy was almost apoplectic.

"We shall be married in Washington," said Kalora decisively. "I am not going to be carted over to my husband's house and delivered at the back door, even if it is the custom of my native land. I shall be married publicly and have twelve bridesmaids."

"You may start for Washington immediately," said her father with genuine enthusiasm.

"I shall need a chaperon. Send for Popova."

"Good! His punishment shall be - permanent exile."

"Nothing would please him better," said Kalora. "Over here he is nothing - in Washington he will be a distinguished foreigner. Washington! *Washington*! To think that all of us are going back there! To think that once more I shall have pickles - all the pickles I want to eat!"

"We have over fifty varieties waiting for you," observed young Mr. Pike tenderly.

"I have been thinking," spoke up the Governor-General. "I shall apply to the Sultan. He shall make you a Most Noble Prince of the Order of Bosporus. The decoration is a great star, studded with diamonds."

"Thanks," replied Mr. Pike.

That night the great palace at Morovenia was

completely illuminated for the first time in many
months.

www.ingramcontent.com/pod-product-compliance
Lightning Source LLC
Chambersburg PA
CBHW031852170626
46807CB00004B/1685